Table of Contents

The Spelling Bee Story

RICKY VARGAS:
The Funniest Kid in the World

Egg-stra funny!

by Alan Katz

with illustrations by Stacy Curtis

LITTLE APPLE

Scholastic Inc.

New York   Toronto   London   Auckland   Sydney   Mexico City   New Delhi   Hong Kong

Ricky Vargas is seven.

He is in second grade.

And he is funny.

Very funny.

Very, very, very funny.

So funny, he makes people
snort milk out of their noses.

Even when they're not
drinking milk.

Now *that's* funny.

Ricky is funny in the school yard....

Ricky is funny in class...

...like when his teacher
asked Ricky if he had a note from
his mother.

Ricky said, "Yes, Mrs. Wilder, I do!"

Then he took a deep breath and sang...
"Laaaaaaa..."

"That's a fine note." Mrs. Wilder
smiled. "But not the one I want."

"Okay, how about *this* one?" Ricky asked.

"Faaaaaaaa..."

Ricky is funny in gym....

At home, Ricky always finds
ways to crack up the family....

Ricky is even funny at
the doctor's office....

"Hello, Dr. Nelson," Ricky said.

He opened his mouth.

Then he stuck out his tongue
as far as it would go.

People always think
Ricky is a riot.

Of course, there are times
that Ricky gets so busy making
everyone laugh, he loses track of
what he really should be
doing.

That happened last week—
at the Spelling Bee....

Ricky's pal Eddie had scored by
spelling TOWEL, so their class
was only one point behind. It was
Ricky's turn, and he knew it
was a big moment.

Everyone was quiet.

Miss Young said, "Ricky, your word is FOR–"

Ricky jumped right in.

He said, "Well, there's F-O-R, as in, 'a gift *for* me!'
F-O-U-R, that's the number four.

There's F-O-R-E like in golf!
Fore!

"Wow, what a great shot!
Ricky Vargas gets a hole in one!
O-N-E!
And he won! W-O-N!"

"There's also T-W-O, T-O, and T-O-O!
Plus E-I-G-H-T, which is one more
than seven.
Also A-T-E like I *ate* a pie...."

Ricky went on for a long time.
A *really* long time.

At first, his teammates were
laughing. But it wasn't so funny
when Miss Young said...

Ricky froze.

His whole team froze.

Miss Young said, "Zero points!"

Because Ricky's spelling word
wasn't FOR.

It was...FORGOT.

Ricky had gone too far.

And because of him,
his team lost.

L-O-S-T.

No one laughed at Ricky
the rest of the day.

TODAY'S FRENCH WORDS:

HAT = CHAPEAU
GIVE = DONNER
DOG = CHIEN

Well, maybe they did...*a little*.

You see, Ricky Vargas knows
what to do when he's made
a mistake.

And after all, he *is* the funniest kid
in the world.

The Class Picture Story

"Good morning, class,"
said Mrs. Wilder on a very, very, very, very
rainy day.

"I am glad everyone made it
to school on this very, very,
very rainy day," she added.

"You forgot one *very*," said
Ricky, pointing to the words
above her head.

"Yes, Ricky, it is a very, very, very, *very* rainy day indeed." Mrs. Wilder smiled. "It is a good day to stay inside!"

"Unless you're a tree!" Ricky said. "Or a llama. Or a moose."

Mrs. Wilder and the whole class
giggled.

They giggled even more
when Mrs. Wilder told Ricky he
was correct, and said, "If there
are any trees, llamas, or moose
in this classroom, please go back
outside right now!"

Mrs. Wilder added, "I am
glad it's raining. That means
we'll have indoor recess,
and you won't get messy or
dirty on this very special day...."

"Does anyone know why today
is so special?"

"No, Ricky...it's Class Picture
Day," the teacher said.
"So practice your very best
smiles for the camera."

And that's just what they did.

For a long time.

A *long* time.

Then the class had its
usual day of math and science
and reading and French lessons.

Mrs. Wilder kept telling the
students to stay neat and clean
for the pictures.

But at recess, Eddie got a bump
on his forehead when he
tried to knock down all the pins
by sliding into them....

Ricky helped him up and said,
"Eddie, you just got a spare.
Too bad you don't have
a spare *head*!"

At lunch, Kiera spilled a whole
cup of blueberry yogurt
on her new red-and-white sweater.

By the end of the day, Eddie's
bump was better and Mrs. Wilder
had carefully helped Kiera
turn her sweater around so the
yogurt wouldn't be seen.

Everyone lined up in the gym for
the class picture.

"Okay, I want big smiles," said
Miss Verdi, who was taking the
pictures for the school.

"Everybody say, 'No homework!'"
Ricky told the group.

"Nice try, Ricky," Mrs. Wilder said.
But saying 'Cheese' will be just fine."

"One...

...two..."

"CHEESE!"

A few days later, the class pictures came.
Everyone was very, very, very, very excited!
No one could tell Eddie had a bump. No one
could tell Kiera was wearing a cup of yogurt
on the back of her sweater.

But *everyone* could see Ricky trying to make a funny face—but at the worst possible time. Which didn't make anyone laugh.

S. WILDER'S CLASS
SECOND GRADE

Ricky said, "I'm sorry"
either 214 or 215 times.
(Eddie counted, and he wasn't sure
if number 108 was an
"I'm sorry" or a sneeze.)
But Ricky knew he had to do more.

That night, Ricky used the
family computer and found a
nice, smiling picture of himself.
He printed 22 copies on sticker paper,
cut them out, and brought them
to school the next day.

It was a perfect fit! Now everyone's class picture had a good shot of Ricky.

And Ricky learned an important lesson: It's okay to make funny faces on "one" and "two..."

The Vargish Story

"I can't believe we have French homework," Eddie moaned as he and Ricky walked home from school.

"Listen, we're lucky," said Ricky. "In Paris, kids have to do all of their homework in French!"

"Math is in French, science is in French..."

"I get it!" said Eddie.

"...they even have to take Spanish lessons in French!" added Ricky.

"That's ridiculous," said Eddie.

"Hey, it's not my idea," Ricky
told him.

Ricky and Eddie were best friends
and next-door neighbors.

Except when they were mad at
each other.

In that case, they weren't best
friends for a little while, but
they were still next-door neighbors
(because it was too hard to move
every time they had a fight).

Eddie liked laughing along with
Ricky. But he didn't know what
to do when Ricky said...

I think
it's time to
start my own
language!

That night, Ricky worked and
worked and worked and worked,
and after five minutes, he had
come up with a whole new way
of speaking.

Meow? Meow!
Meow, purr purr,
meow! Ha!

It wasn't English.

It wasn't French.

It wasn't anything anyone had
ever heard before.

It was...

VARGISH!

"Good morning, Ricky," said
Mrs. Wilder.

Mrs. Wilder knew something
was up, because that was a
strange answer, even for Ricky.

"He is speaking Vargish,"
Eddie said to the teacher.
"It's his new language."

"Ricky, greb num pla pla
delp!" Mrs. Wilder said.

She was trying to say, "Please
stop talking that way."

But she didn't really know Vargish.

65

Even the teachers were speaking it.

Vargish was taking over the whole school!

And guess what happened next....

Kaba blee blee demby voo!

Oops!

What happened was
Ricky stood up and shouted...

WHAT IN THE WORLD ARE YOU ALL TALKING ABOUT?

And just like that, the teachers
and students all went back
to speaking English.

And everything was exactly as it had been before.

Well, almost everything...

"I can't believe we have Vargish homework," Eddie moaned as he and Ricky walked home from school.

SMACK!